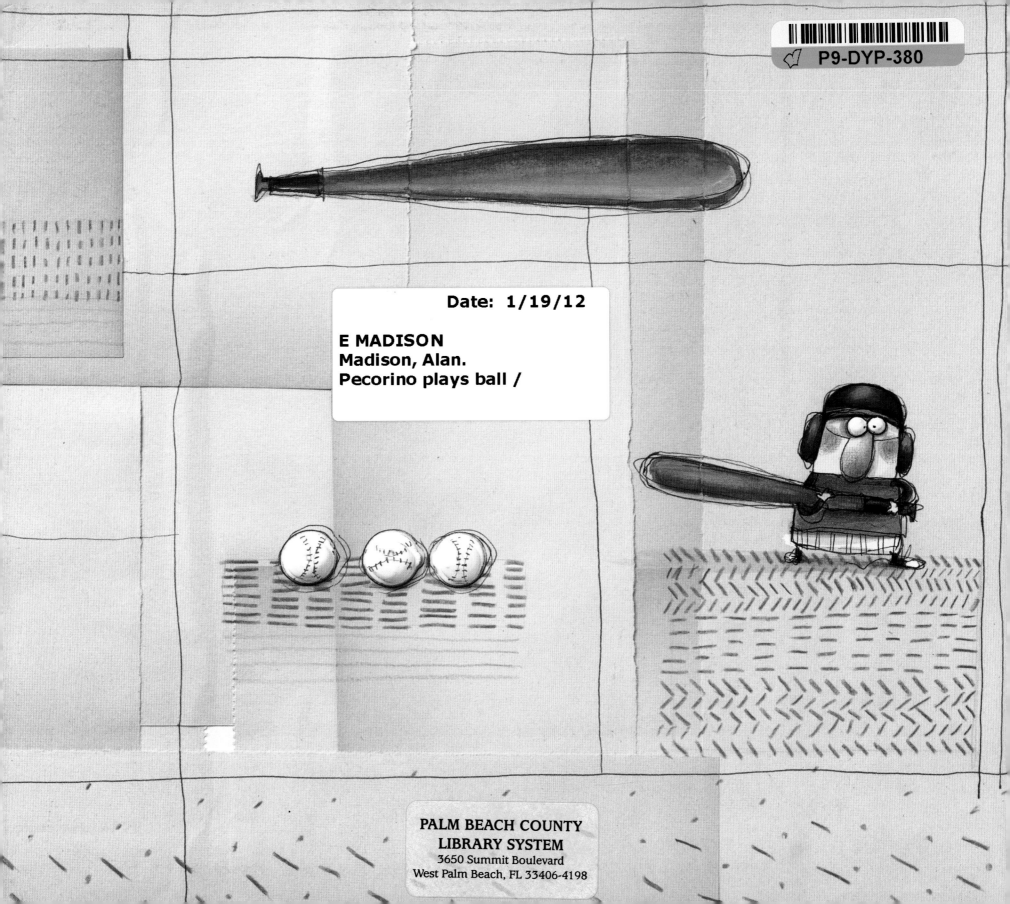

P9-DYP-380

Date: 1/19/12

E MADISON
Madison, Alan.
Pecorino plays ball /

PALM BEACH COUNTY
LIBRARY SYSTEM
3650 Summit Boulevard
West Palm Beach, FL 33406-4198

Atheneum Books for Young Readers
An imprint of Simon & Schuster Children's
Publishing Division
1230 Avenue of the Americas
New York, New York 10020
Text copyright © 2006 by Alan Madison
Illustrations copyright © 2006
by AnnaLaura Cantone
All rights reserved, including the right of
reproduction in whole or in part in any form.
Book design by Jessica Sonkin
The text for this book is set in Graham.
The illustrations are rendered in acrylic, pen,
pencil, and collage.
Manufactured in China
First Edition
10 9 8 7 6 5 4 3 2 1
Library of Congress Cataloging-in-Publication Data
Madison, Alan.
Pecorino plays ball / Alan Madison ; illustrated
by AnnaLaura Cantone.—1st ed.
p. cm.
"An Anne Schwartz Book."
Summary: Pecorino Sasquatch proves that he
is still the silliest boy in the world when his first
day of Little League arrives and he realizes he
has never hit or caught a baseball before—nor
even chewed bubble gum.
ISBN-13: 978-0-689-86522-0
ISBN-10: 0-689-86522-8
[1. Baseball—Fiction. 2. Humorous stories.]
I. Cantone, AnnaLaura, ill. II. Title.
PZ7.M2587Pe 2006
[E]—dc21   2003004219

For Caleb, who continues to teach me the true
grace of the game.
To my parents, for raising me silly and making
sure I was well red and not purrpull.
And to the kind parents who continue kind
coaching for the West Side Little League.
—A. M.

To Jim, who almost always
has answers for my "whys"
and "what does it means,"
with love
—A. C.

PECORINO
PLAYS BALL

by Alan Madison

Illustrated by
AnnaLaura Cantone

AN ANNE SCHWARTZ BOOK
Atheneum Books for Young Readers · New York · London · Toronto · Sydney

Everyone thought Pecorino Sasquatch was the silliest boy in the whole wide world. He was so silly that he would wear slippers in a snowstorm and boots in a bath. He was so silly, he would eat candy on Thanksgiving and turkey on Halloween.

One fine sparkling morn Pecorino's mother awoke him, announcing, "Dearest dumpling, today is a special spring Saturday! It is your first day of Little League!" Pecorino was so excited, he sprung out of bed and sprang to his window. It was beautiful outside—the trees were singing and the birds were budding.

"Wait a spring second," moaned Pecorino. "What's *Little League*?"
"Little League," explained his mother, "is when children on one team play baseball against children on another team."

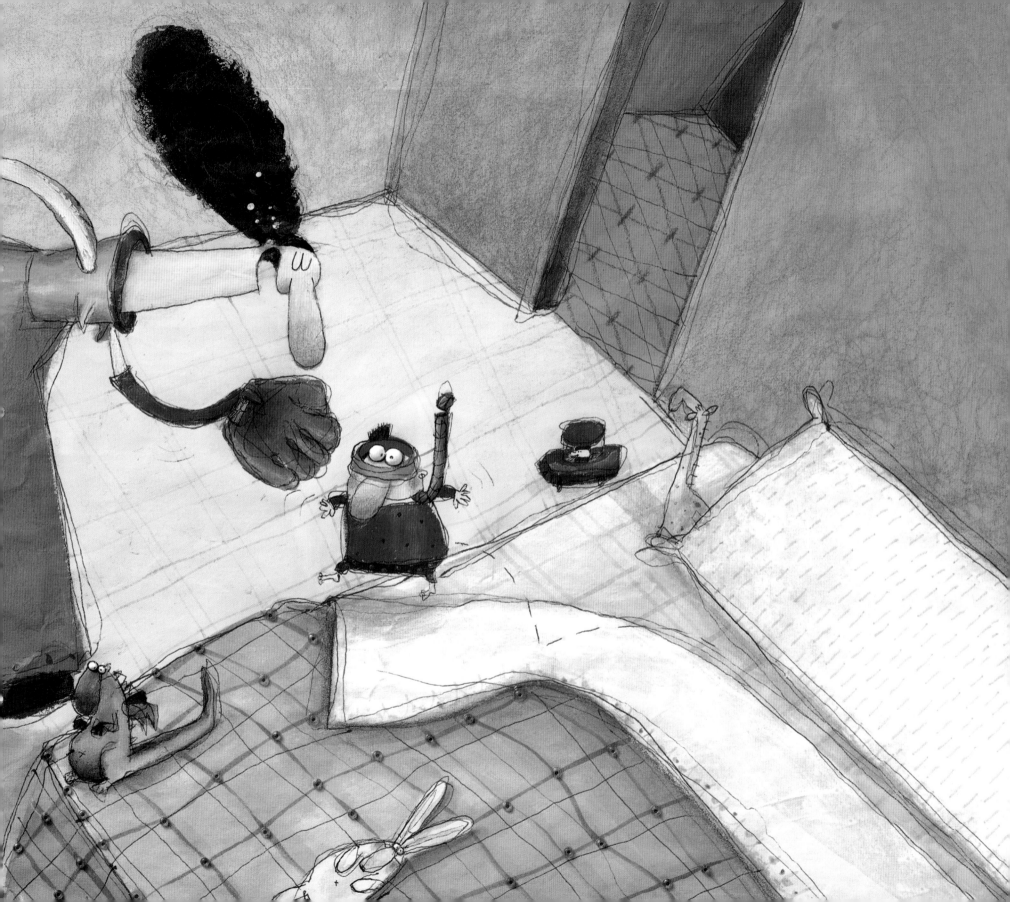

From the edge of the field in the great green park,
they watched boys and girls in tiger orange shirts
scoop, scatch, and scorch baseballs.

Mrs. Sasquatch gave Pecorino a peck
on the cheek, whispered, "Have fun," and
sidestepped over to the other grown-ups.

"Coach Credenza is my name
and baseball is my game,"
boomed a big voice from above.
The massive man, shaped like a bowling
pin with a small head and a wide
bottom, eyeballed Pecorino from
toe to top, then teetered to hand
him the very last orange shirt.

13

Pecorino slid into the Xtra-Xtra-large uniform. Boxy black letters crossed his chest and dropped to his sneaker tops. Upside down he read:

**ALONE
WE SELL
OXES**

Pecorino worried that instead of playing baseball like the others, he would be selling big blue Bunyanesque oxes.

Two teammates, gum bubbles burbling off their lips, stared at Pecorino. They wore orange shirts exactly like his except theirs read:

MALONE'S
WE SELL
BOXES

Pecorino slowly lifted one arm. Hiding underneath was a capital *M*, and on his hip hid a big *B*. Then he lifted his other arm and there was a little *s*.

"Ohhhh!" exclaimed Pecorino.
"We don't sell oxes.
We sell boxes!!"

And the gum burblers scuttled away.

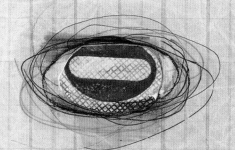

As Pecorino scuttled after them, he stepped on the tiger orange tail of his Xtra-large, Xtra-long shirt, tripped, and somersaulted into the grass.

"Tuck it in," commanded Coach Credenza.

He tucked and tucked, until "We Sell Oxes"
disappeared below his belt, and all that was left
written across his belly was:

ALONE

"The Malone's don't lose," graveled the coach, pointing Pecorino to right field. "If a ball comes, you better catch it."

There was one problem, thought Pecorino as he rambled to right—he had never actually caught a baseball.

The pitcher pitched. The batter swung.
The bat cracked. Pecorino looked up, but all he saw
were cottony clouds. The white pill of a ball hopped to one
of the gum-burbling boys, who scooped it, then scorched it to the
other gum burbler, who scatched it right up.
"Yer out!" howled the umpire, hitchhiking his thick thumb to the sky.
Pecorino imagined himself burbling bubbles, scooping, and scorching, but there were
two problems—he didn't have any gum, and he had never caught a baseball.

After three "Yer outs" it was his team's turn to bat. A boy blowing a small pink balloon of a bubble jogged out to take Pecorino's spot in right field. Scripty red letters crossed his chest and dropped to his sneaker tops. Pecorino read out loud:

"hit
me
ear."

The boy popped his bubble and stretched his arms up as he passed. Now his shirt read:

White's
Women's
Wear

"Better tuck it in," advised Pecorino.
The boy tucked and tucked, until the "ear," which used to be "Wear," disappeared below his belt. And written across his belly was:

hit

me

Big bat on his shoulder, Pecorino crouched over home plate.
"The Boxes don't lose," Coach Credenza boiled.

"If a ball comes, you better hit it."

Now there were three problems.
Pecorino counted:

1. he didn't have any gum;

2. he had never caught a baseball; and

3. he had certainly never hit one.

"Strike ONE!" the umpire bellowed as the blur of a ball zippered by.
Pecorino squinted his eyes and saw Hit Me standing way away, where he wished he was.

"Strike TWO!" The blur-ball smacked into the catcher's glove.

Pecorino needed to swing, and hard. He gritted his teeth and gathered all his strength from his ankles to his eyeballs. The pitcher pitched.
Pecorino swung . . . and missed.

"Yer out!" yodeled the ump, throwing that thick thumb over his shoulder.

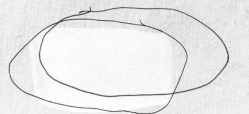

Coach shook his head, the gum burblers shook their heads, the whole ALONE WE SELL OXES team shook their heads.

Pecorino ran straight out to right field, and Hit Me ran straight in.
Near first base their paths crossed. Hit Me nodded nicely.

Pressed into the grass where
Hit Me had just stood were his two
peanut-shaped footprints, and at
the center of each was a single
square of bubble gum.

Pecorino popped the gooey gifts into
his mouth and started to chomp.
One problem solved,
he chewed. Now all
he had to do was
hit and catch
the ball.

"Yer out!" yapped the umpire three more times. Pecorino ran to the dugout, and as he passed Hit Me, he called, "Thank you." But because the gum cloggered his mouth, it sounded like "Ack—oh." Which made Hit Me think Pecorino was an Eskimo.

After every set of three "Yer outs" Pecorino ran from right field to the dugout or from the dugout to right field, passing Hit Me going the opposite way. So far neither had tipped, tapped, or touched the ball with their bats, nor had they caught, corralled, or clipped the ball with their mitts.

Coach Credenza cornered Pecorino. "This is it. Last licks," he woofed. "We are winning by one single run. If a ball comes your way, you better catch it."

Still there was that one big problem. . . .

Standing way out in right field, Pecorino was far
from home. He stepped into Hit Me's peanutty prints pressed
in the grass and started to burble a bubble.

Hit Me lifted his bat and stepped to the plate. There were two
outs. If he struck out, Malone's would win the game.

"Striiiiike one!" screeched the umpire.

A teeny, tingly feeling crept up Pecorino's back and got bigger
as it slithered up his neck. Pecorino
wanted Hit Me to hit the ball.

"Striiiiike two!"

Hit Me's head slunkered down. Pecorino wanted Hit Me to bash the ball, because, just like Pecorino, he hadn't touched it at all.

Hit Me waggled the wood. The pitcher pitched the pill. The ump flexed his thumb.

"Strriii . . ."

"Swing," pleaded Pecorino.

And Hit Me swung. The bat cracked! The ball flew!

Pecorino looked up, but all he saw were cottony clouds. Then he saw it. The baseball was flying right toward him. Now there was only one problem. He had never actually . . .

Pecorino raised his mitt over his head. His Xtra-large, Xtra-long shirt pulled out from under his belt, and "MALONE'S WE SELL BOXES" unfurled to his feet. Hit Me rattlesnaked around second. Down came the ball. Back and back pedaled Pecorino. Back and back, until . . . he stepped on the tiger orange tail of his Xtra-large, Xtra-long shirt, tripped, spattled the glob of gum out of his mouth, and tumbled hard onto the grassy ground. The ball spilled down from the clouds, mashed into his mitt, . . .

and stuck.

Silence. So much silence Pecorino thought he might be asleep.

Then Coach Credenza, Mrs. Sasquatch, the burbling boys, and the whole rest of the WE SELL OXES team let out a wildebeest whoop. They had won!

Hit Me staggered past, his head slouched so far down that his chin rested on his belt. "You caught it, Alone," he said. "Not alone at all—you helped," Pecorino reminded him. Hit Me chewed this over, nodded nicely, and smiled.

The red ball of a sun set behind
the singing trees and budding birds.
Mrs. Sasquatch gave Pecorino a kiss on the cheek.
    "Have fun?" she asked.
    "I definitely did," he answered.
    And hand in hand they walked the great green park toward home—not the plate.